BiG PET DaY

For David and Nicole, with love and thanks,
for all the years of fun and chaos! – L.S.

For Isabel. I'm sure SHE could tame a dragon. – GG.

A TEMPLAR BOOK

Published in the UK in 2015 by Templar Publishing,
an imprint of The Templar Company Limited,
Deepdene Lodge, Deepdene Avenue, Dorking, Surrey, RH5 4AT, UK
www.templarco.co.uk

Big Pet Day was first published in Australia by Hachette Australia.
This edition is published by arrangement with Hachette Australia Pty Ltd.

1 3 5 7 9 10 8 6 4 2

ISBN 978-1-78370-201-5 (hardback)
ISBN 978-1-78370-202-2 (softback)

Designed by Ingrid Kwong and Gus Gordon

Printed in China

BiG PET Day

by LisA SHanahaN
illustrations by
gus gordoN

templar publishing
www.templarco.co.uk

Today is Pet Day
in Lily's class.

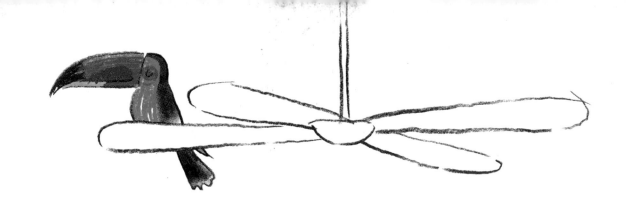

Courtney is trying to make her hermit crabs come out.
Ahmed is whistling at his peach-faced parrots.
Ming is stroking her grey mouse.
Caleb's puppy is chewing his tail.
Sofia's duck is waddling on the mat.
Mrs Dalton is chasing Glen's ferret.

Lily is singing to her dragon.

Mrs Dalton catches Glen's ferret in the dress-up corner and sticky-tapes him back into his box. She wants to keep the classroom tidy because Mr Fisher, the head teacher, is coming later to judge the best pet.

'Excuse me, Mrs Dalton,' says
Courtney. 'Jody's pony is at
the door and it just did a poo!'
Mrs Dalton rests her head.
'What is happening to our
best pet behaviour?'

Lily puts up her hand.
'When my dragon burps,' she says,
'he always covers his mouth.'

'There's no such thing
as dragons,' says Courtney.

After Mrs Dalton cleans up, everyone sits
on the mat and talks about their pets.

'My hermit crabs like to move house,' says Courtney.

'My parrots like kissing,' says Ahmed.

'We thought our mouse was a boy,' says Ming,
'until she had twelve babies.'

'My dog likes to chew on my dad's pants,' says Caleb.

'My duck swims with me in the bath,' says Sofia.

'My ferret sleeps in the
washing machine,' says Glen.

'My pony was in
the circus,' says Jody.

'My dragon tells
great jokes,' says Lily.

'Dragons are only in
fairy tales,' says Courtney.

'I had a pet like Lily's when I was a little girl,'
says Mrs Dalton. 'An aardvark called Annie.'
Everyone rolls around and laughs at the idea
of Mrs Dalton being a little girl.

At playtime, Caleb's puppy and Glen have a dried dog food eating competition.

Mrs Dalton darts across the playground. 'Yoo-hoo!' she calls.

'What is your puppy eating?'

'Half a bag of dog food,' says Caleb, with a small grin.

'And Glen's big bottle of juice,' says Courtney.

'Oh, my word!' cries Mrs Dalton. 'He'll be sick!'

'My dragon never gets sick,' says Lily. 'But he does like cough sweets. Even though he doesn't have a cough.'

'You're making that up,' says Courtney.

After playtime, everyone sits at their desk and draws a picture of their pet. When the pictures are finished, Mrs Dalton tacks them up. 'Who do you think looks most like their pet?' she asks.

The whole class votes for Jody and her pony,

then Glen and his ferret,

then Sofia and her duck.

But **everyone** loves Lily's picture best.

At lunch, Jody's pony does tricks in the playground. She can count to three with her hoof and spin a hula-hoop at the same time.

Ming's mouse dives into her pocket and brings out some cheese.
Caleb's puppy plays football.
Sofia's duck drinks from the water fountain.
Glen's ferret dances on the library steps.

'Look,' says Lily. 'My dragon can write my name in the sky.'
'Wow!' says Glen.

'That's just a cloud,' says Courtney.

After lunch, everyone gets ready
for the Grand Parade.
'Now! Don't forget Mr Fisher
is coming!' cries Mrs Dalton.

Courtney lines up her crabs like soldiers.
Ahmed polishes the mirror in his parrots' cage.
Ming fluffs the fur around her mouse's ears.
Caleb clips on his puppy's best collar.

Sofia sprays her duck with some water.
Glen's ferret wears a sparkly bow tie.
Jody braids her pony's tail with ribbons.
Lily whispers a story to calm her dragon's nerves.

Then Mr Fisher, the head teacher, is there with his loud, crunchy voice and his stiff, woolly hair. He hugs a big gold trophy while the whole class parades around the room.

But Glen trips!

e e e e e e e e e ee k k k!

Mr Fisher screams and screams as five
tiny hermit crabs skitter about his feet.

Lily's dragon roars.

And roars.

roaAArrr!

And roars!

Until everything is *quiet*.

'Oooh!' breathes Mr Fisher.

'Ooh!' gasps Courtney.

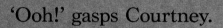

'Oh!' sighs Mrs Dalton, with a smile.
'Thank you!'

After Mrs Dalton searches out every last hermit crab, the whole class sits on the mat and votes with Mr Fisher.

And everyone cheers when Lily's dragon wins the big gold trophy for best pet.